Tyler Is Out of Bounds!

And Other Really Good Reasons to CHOOSE WISELY

Kirkland street.

FaithKiDs

Written and illustrated by
Sandy Silverthorne

In memory of my mom:
You always knew I could do stuff like this.
Thanks for teaching me to be obedient.

Faith Kids™ is an imprint of
Cook Communications Ministries,
Colorado Springs, Colorado 80918
Cook Communications, Paris, Ontario
Kingsway Communications, Eastbourne, England

TYLER IS OUT OF BOUNDS!
© 2000 by Sandy Silverthorne for text and illustrations

Designed by iDesignEtc.
Edited by Kathy Davis
Design direction by Kelly S. Robinson

First hardcover printing, 2000
Printed in the United States of America
 04 03 02 01 00   5 4 3 2 1

Library of Congress Cataloging-in-Publication Data

Silverthorne, Sandy, 1951-
        Tyler is out of bounds! : and other really good reasons to choose wisely /
        by Sandy Silverthorne.
                p. cm. — (Kirkland Street kids)
        Summary: Tyler has been naughty, but his Sunday school teacher explains that
following God's rules will help him behave better.
        ISBN 0-7814-3294-4
        [1. Behavior—Fiction. 2. Christian life—Fiction.]
I. Title.
PZ7.S5884 Ty 2000
[E]—dc21

                                                                99-044724

7:00 A.M.

The whole house was quiet . . . except for the sound of
Choo-Choo Puffies being poured into a bowl.

Choo-Choo Puffies was a presweetened, fruit-flavored cereal shaped like little locomotives, boxcars, and cabooses. It was Jamie's favorite.

Every morning he'd pour a bowl, get some orange juice and a muffin, and sit down to "The Breakfast of Railroaders."

What Jamie didn't notice this morning was the shadowy figure lurking behind the kitchen door.

As soon as Jamie got up to get the funnies, the shadowy figure made his move.

As quick as a flash, he darted out from his hiding place, streaked across the room, and swooped up Jamie's cereal.

Before Jamie knew what was happening, the thief, Jamie's older brother Tyler, was sitting on the sofa finishing off Jamie's cereal.

Tyler had been like this lately—mean and selfish. It was as if there were two Tylers. There was the Good Tyler who was nice, kind, and thoughtful ...

... then there was the Naughty Tyler who made everybody's life miserable.

Nobody had seen much of the nice Tyler lately.

That day at school, Naughty Tyler got into trouble for cutting in line, looking at Marpel's test paper, calling Gregory a geek, and standing on his chair.

And that was all before lunch.

It was as if Naughty Tyler had completely taken over.

What?

Of course, we all have a naughty side that wants to do bad stuff, but when Naughty Tyler and Naughty Bradley got together with Naughty Gregory, Naughty Christy, and Naughty Marpel on the playground it got pretty crowded... and pretty unpleasant.

At Sunday school that week it appeared that Mr. Fleece had noticed this whole good-kid/bad-kid routine because the lesson was on obedience.

Tyler liked Mr. Fleece. He made Sunday school fun.

Once he dressed up like a whale for the story of Jonah. Another time he played Moses when they talked about the Ten Commandments.

(His beard looked funny and you could tell it was his bathrobe, but he made a good Moses anyway.)

Now Mr. Fleece stood in front of the class with two puppets he'd made. They both looked like him!

"The Bible talks about our old self that wants to do bad things, and our new self that wants to follow Jesus and do what's right."

Naughty Tyler didn't like where this was going.

Mr. Fleece continued, "So the more you do what's right, the stronger your new self will become."

The kids liked this idea, and Mr. Fleece assured them that Jesus would help them do this each day.

"Too bad you always forget everything you hear in Sunday school," Naughty Tyler said as they left the class.

The next morning the only sound you could hear was Jamie pouring his bowl of Choo-Choo Puffies. And what was this? The prize! The cube puzzle from Engineer Carl.

Whoa! Jamie knew there had only been four or five million of these ever made! They were a collector's item!

As Jamie turned to get some orange juice, it happened again—the streak through the kitchen, the pounce. His cereal—*and the prize*—were history!

This time when Jamie called his mom he had tears in his eyes.

This wasn't funny anymore.

Tyler spent most of that day in his room.

When he was released, Tyler decided it was time to talk to Mr. Fleece.

"No, don't go to his house! He's probably not even home!" shouted Naughty Tyler as they rounded the corner to Mr. Fleece's house.

"He's always given you good advice in the past," said Good Tyler.

"What's to say he'll be right this time?" sneered Naughty Tyler.

Mr. Fleece was in his front yard. He and Tyler sat down on the steps.

For once Naughty Tyler was quiet. "It's like I have these two Tylers inside of me," Tyler explained. "Does that go away when you get older?"

"Afraid not," said Mr. Fleece.

"Does that sound crazy?" Tyler asked.

"Not at all," said Mr. Fleece. "You have an old self, the naughty Tyler, and the new self, the good Tyler—the one God's working on. Remember when you gave your life to Jesus?"

"Of course. It was last summer at day camp. That's why I can't figure out why I'm still bad sometimes," Tyler replied.

"Living your life with Jesus doesn't mean you'll never do wrong things," Mr. Fleece explained. "It just means Jesus is always with you and He'll help you in every situation."

"But there seem to be so many rules. Why do we need all those rules, anyway?" asked Tyler, who was feeling more hopeless by the minute.

"Let me show you," said Mr. Fleece as he rose and disappeared into the house.

In just a minute he appeared with his puppy, Max. Mr. Fleece put the puppy down on the grass. "Is Max safe from traffic here in the yard?" he asked.

"Yeah," Tyler replied. "He's got that fence to keep him in."

"What if I put him out on the sidewalk?" asked Mr. Fleece.

"No! Don't do it. He'll run into the street and get hit by a car!" shouted Tyler.

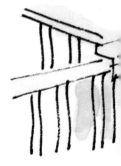

"Tyler, **God's rules are like** this fence. They're here to protect us and others. If we stay within the fence we'll be safe—and so will the people around us," Mr. Fleece explained.

"That makes a lot of sense," said Good Tyler, who was feeling stronger by the minute.

Talking to Mr. Fleece always made Tyler think. And think. And think. He really wanted to do the right thing, but it was sooooo hard.

Tyler decided to ask God to help him make right choices.

7:00 the next morning. The only sound in the house was the clatter of Choo-Choo Puffies being poured into a bowl. But this time it was Tyler pouring them for Jamie, who wasn't up yet.

"I can't believe you're doing this," groaned Naughty Tyler as he lay on the kitchen floor.

"Quiet," said Good Tyler as he scooped up the funnies and headed for Jamie's room. "My little brother deserves breakfast in bed on occasion."

Faith Parenting Guide

Tyler Is Out of Bounds!
And Other Really Good Reasons to Choose Wisely

Ages: 4-7

Life Issue: I want my child to learn to choose wisely.

Spiritual Building Block: Wisdom

Learning Styles

Sight: Ask your child if she has ever felt like Tyler—with two different sets of desires (for example: wanting to share and then snatching). Take two pairs of your child's shoes—one that fits well and one that is too small (another type of clothing will do). Explain that choosing wisely is like putting on the shoes that fit—you want to wear them, they help you get where you need to go, and they feel good. Choosing unwisely (disobedience) is like putting on the smaller shoes—it hurts you and it sure doesn't make you want to go very far. Unwise choices hinder you in life. Obeying God always fits just right and gives God's protection—just as the fence protects the puppy in the story.

Sound: Read aloud the Parable of the Prodigal Son in a child's Bible. Two sons each made a choice—one wise and one unwise. What happened when the prodigal realized he'd made a poor choice and lost everything? Read Luke 2:52: "And Jesus grew in wisdom and stature, and in favor with God and men." Ask your child why he thinks Jesus needed to *grow* in wisdom.

Touch: Cut six card pieces out of a poster board. Mark three with the word wisdom and three with the word folly. On the backs, put three simple "proverbs" that pertain to wisdom and folly (for example: "The Lord blesses busy hands."). Then throw the cards in a hat and let your child pick them one at a time. Read the card to her and ask if this idea is wise or unwise. Encourage your child to make her own cards with her very own "proverbs" (for example: "Always brush your teeth after you eat pickles"—*wisdom!* or "Eat dessert before your meat and vegetables"—*folly!*).